W9-ANW-838

Hero Tales

LITTLE, BROWN & COMPANY
LB kids

HASBRO and its logo, TRANSFORMERS, RESCUE BOTS and all related characters are trademarks of Hasbro and are used with permission. © 2017 Hasbro. All Rights Reserved.

Transformers Rescue Bots: Meet Griffin Rock Rescue: Character Guide originally published in June 2016 by LB kids
Transformers Rescue Bots: The Ghosts of Griffin Rock originally published in September 2014 by LB kids
Transformers Rescue Bots: Land Before Prime originally published in January 2015 by LB kids
Transformers Rescue Bots: Blast Off! originally published in June 2015 by LB kids
Transformers Rescue Bots: Race to the Rescue originally published in November 2016 by LB kids
Transformers Rescue Bots: Dangerous Rescue originally published in January 2016 by LB kids

Cover design by Elaine Lopez-Levine.

Hachette Book Group supports the right to free expression and the value of copyright. The purpose of copyright is to encourage writers and artists to produce the creative works that enrich our culture.

The scanning, uploading, and distribution of this book without permission is a theft of the author's intellectual property. If you would like permission to use material from the book (other than for review purposes), please contact permissions@hbgusa.com. Thank you for your support of the author's rights.

Little, Brown and Company

Hachette Book Group
1290 Avenue of the Americas, New York, NY 10104
Visit us at LBYR.com

First Bindup Edition: November 2017

LB kids is an imprint of Little, Brown and Company. The LB kids name and logo are trademarks of Hachette Book Group, Inc.

The publisher is not responsible for websites (or their content) that are not owned by the publisher.

ISBNs: 978-0-316-48016-1 (hardcover)

Printed in China

RRD-S

10 9 8 7 6 5 4 3 2 1

Licensed By:

Table of Contents

TRANSFORMERS RESCUE BOTS

Meet Griffin Rock Rescue Character Guide

By Steve Foxe

LITTLE, BROWN & COMPANY
LB kids

The Rescue Bots are a special group of Transformers sworn to serve and protect the human race. The first Rescue Bots were part of Rescue Force Sigma-17. Their spaceship drifted through space until Optimus Prime called them to Earth. The Autobot leader ordered the Rescue Bots to live and work with a human family on the island of Griffin Rock, Maine. They all help keep the planet safe!

GRIFFIN ROCK

The town of Griffin Rock is home to many scientists who test strange, new gadgets on the island. Though most of these experiments eventually benefit all humankind, some do go awry. Good thing the Rescue Bots are always on call!

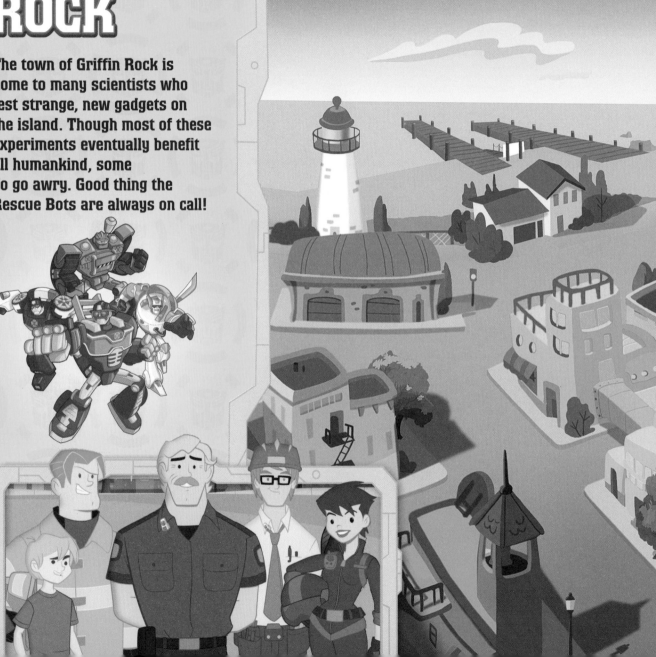

4

RESCUE HEADQUARTERS

The Rescue Bots and their human partners detect these disasters from Rescue Headquarters, Griffin Rock's fire station. Whenever trouble pops up, the Rescue Bots best suited for each mission are deployed. Sometimes all the Rescue Bots must roll to the rescue!

Heatwave

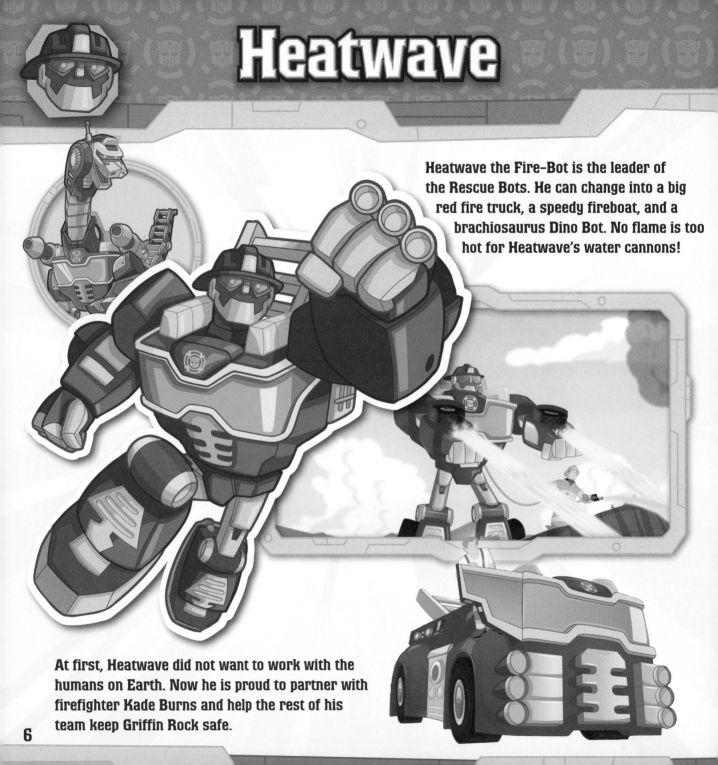

Heatwave the Fire-Bot is the leader of the Rescue Bots. He can change into a big red fire truck, a speedy fireboat, and a brachiosaurus Dino Bot. No flame is too hot for Heatwave's water cannons!

At first, Heatwave did not want to work with the humans on Earth. Now he is proud to partner with firefighter Kade Burns and help the rest of his team keep Griffin Rock safe.

Chase

Chase the Police-Bot loves following the law. He was the first Bot from Rescue Force Sigma-17 to embrace living on Earth. His vehicle mode is a police cruiser with flashing lights and a loud siren.

Chase can also change into a stegosaurus Dino Bot with a spiky tail. He works with Chief Charlie Burns, the human leader of the Rescue Team. Together, they can hunt down any criminal and help stop any disaster.

Boulder

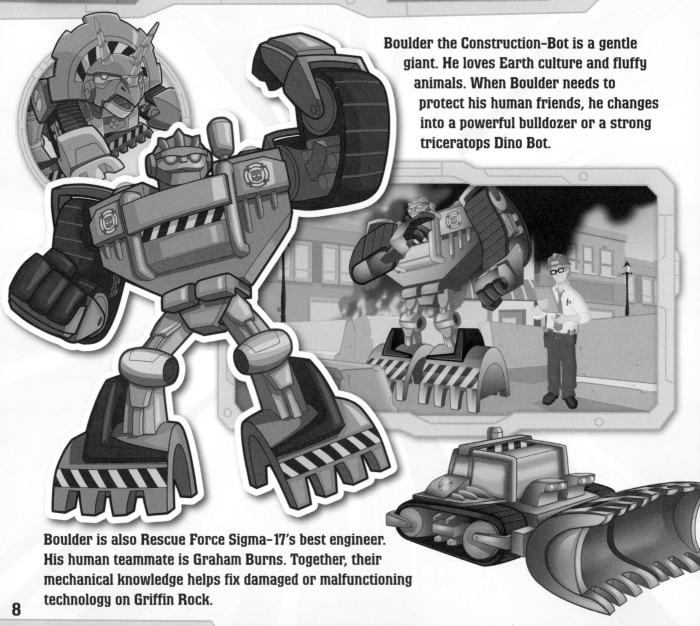

Boulder the Construction-Bot is a gentle giant. He loves Earth culture and fluffy animals. When Boulder needs to protect his human friends, he changes into a powerful bulldozer or a strong triceratops Dino Bot.

Boulder is also Rescue Force Sigma-17's best engineer. His human teammate is Graham Burns. Together, their mechanical knowledge helps fix damaged or malfunctioning technology on Griffin Rock.

Blades

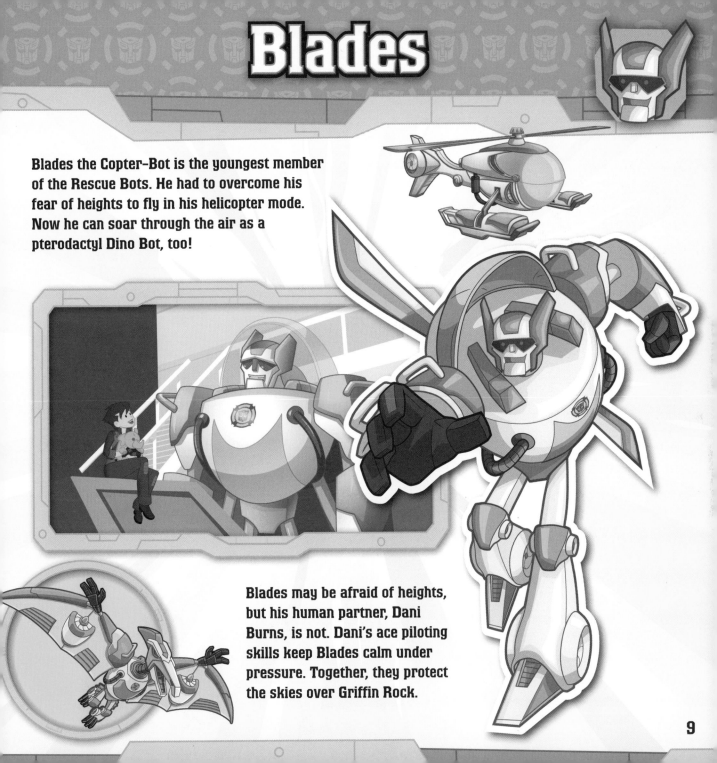

Blades the Copter-Bot is the youngest member of the Rescue Bots. He had to overcome his fear of heights to fly in his helicopter mode. Now he can soar through the air as a pterodactyl Dino Bot, too!

Blades may be afraid of heights, but his human partner, Dani Burns, is not. Dani's ace piloting skills keep Blades calm under pressure. Together, they protect the skies over Griffin Rock.

Bumblebee

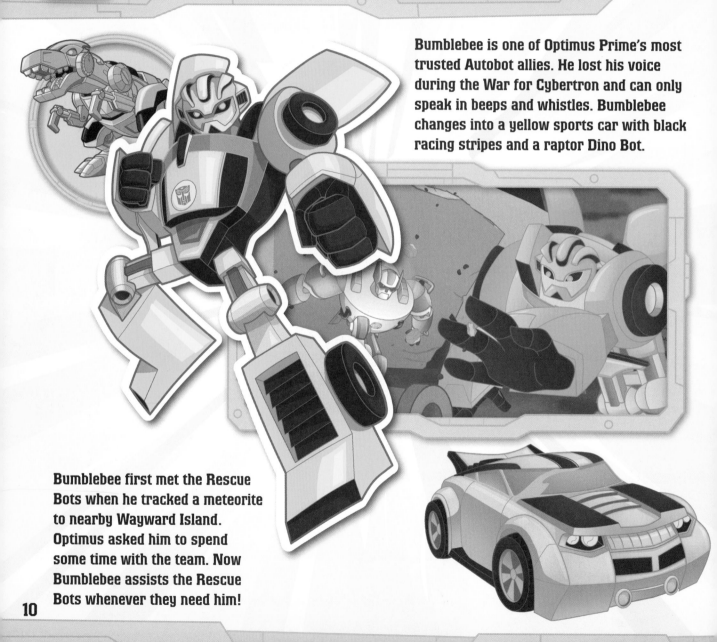

Bumblebee is one of Optimus Prime's most trusted Autobot allies. He lost his voice during the War for Cybertron and can only speak in beeps and whistles. Bumblebee changes into a yellow sports car with black racing stripes and a raptor Dino Bot.

Bumblebee first met the Rescue Bots when he tracked a meteorite to nearby Wayward Island. Optimus asked him to spend some time with the team. Now Bumblebee assists the Rescue Bots whenever they need him!

Optimus Prime

Optimus Prime is the heroic leader of the Autobots. He holds the Matrix of Leadership, an object of great power. Optimus gave the Rescue Bots a mission to live on Earth and protect humans from natural disasters and science gone wrong.

Optimus changes into a blue-and-red semitruck. On a mission to the mysterious Wayward Island, Optimus also gained the ability to change into a mighty Tyrannosaurus rex by scanning Trex, Doc Greene's dinosaur robot!

High Tide

High Tide is a drill instructor with a cranky attitude, but he is one of Optimus Prime's oldest friends. High Tide changes into a submarine to assist with water rescues. If needed, he can also combine with his ship to form a giant Mega-Bot.

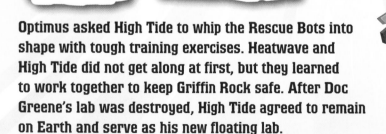

Optimus asked High Tide to whip the Rescue Bots into shape with tough training exercises. Heatwave and High Tide did not get along at first, but they learned to work together to keep Griffin Rock safe. After Doc Greene's lab was destroyed, High Tide agreed to remain on Earth and serve as his new floating lab.

Blurr and his partner, Salvage, crashed onto Earth thousands of years ago during a meteor shower. They slept in stasis until the Rescue Bots found them. Blurr is a purple Autobot who changes into a lightning-fast race car.

Blurr has trouble following orders on Earth. He just wants to race! He even stole the Rescue Bots' spaceship to escape the planet, but he returned it and saved the day in the process. Optimus Prime later gave Blurr and Salvage a mission to start their own Rescue Team away from Griffin Rock.

13

Salvage

Salvage is very different from his companion, Blurr. Where Blurr can be edgy and impatient, Salvage is quiet and calm. He changes into a big green garbage truck and likes to recycle trash and turn forgotten objects into effective rescue tools.

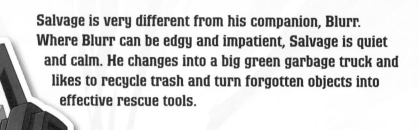

When Blurr stole the Rescue Bots' spaceship to leave Earth, Salvage talked him into returning it. Optimus Prime rewarded Salvage by making him a Rescue Bot. Salvage joined Blurr to lead their own Rescue Bot squad elsewhere.

Trex & Servo

Trex is a Tyrannosaurus rex robot that Doc Greene programmed to guard his lab. When he's not scaring away intruders, Trex makes coffee for his master. Trex has been hacked and forced to turn against the Rescue Bots in the past, but Doc Greene always fixes him. On a mission to Wayward Island, Trex once saved Doc Greene from being crushed by falling rocks.

Servo is High Tide's faithful dog robot. He can change into all sorts of useful things, like a crowbar or a wheelbarrow, and can even be commanded with a dog whistle. When he's not working with the Rescue Bots, Servo enjoys playing fetch with Cody Burns or chasing Mayor Luskey's wife's dog, Poopsie, around Griffin Rock.

Charlie Burns & Cody Burns

Chief Charlie Burns is the human leader of the Rescue Team and the father of Kade, Graham, Dani, and Cody. His Rescue Bot partner is Chase the Police-Bot. Chief Burns uses his rescue tools and years of experience to assist the Bots!

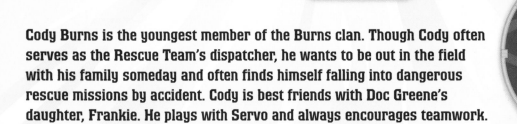

Cody Burns is the youngest member of the Burns clan. Though Cody often serves as the Rescue Team's dispatcher, he wants to be out in the field with his family someday and often finds himself falling into dangerous rescue missions by accident. Cody is best friends with Doc Greene's daughter, Frankie. He plays with Servo and always encourages teamwork.

Kade Burns & Dani Burns

Kade Burns is a firefighter and the oldest Burns sibling. He has a quick temper and often clashes with his Rescue Bot partner, Heatwave. He loves his family, even if he is sometimes a bit mean to his little brother Cody.

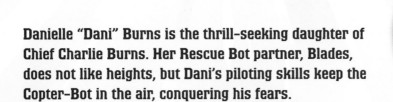

Danielle "Dani" Burns is the thrill-seeking daughter of Chief Charlie Burns. Her Rescue Bot partner, Blades, does not like heights, but Dani's piloting skills keep the Copter-Bot in the air, conquering his fears.

Graham Burns & Woody Burns

Graham Burns loves science and engineering. He lets his siblings Dani and Kade handle most of the action, but he contributes to the team by being the brains behind many missions alongside his partner, Boulder.

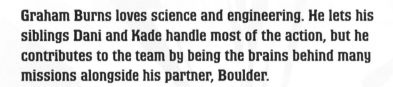

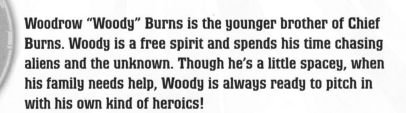

Woodrow "Woody" Burns is the younger brother of Chief Burns. Woody is a free spirit and spends his time chasing aliens and the unknown. Though he's a little spacey, when his family needs help, Woody is always ready to pitch in with his own kind of heroics!

Doc Greene & Frankie Greene

Doc Greene is an eccentric but brilliant scientist who lives in Griffin Rock. His experiments sometimes backfire and cause trouble around the island, keeping the Rescue Bots very busy. The dinosaur robot Trex and the floating helper robot Dither are two of Doc Greene's many inventions. After working together on lots of scientific endeavors, Doc Greene married Professor Baranova.

Francine "Frankie" Greene is Doc Greene's equally brilliant and brave daughter. She is best friends with Cody Burns and likes to accompany the Rescue Bots on missions. She wants to be a scientist like her father and often helps clean up his mistakes.

Mayor Luskey & Huxley Prescott

Mayor Luskey has been the mayor of Griffin Rock for many years. He is married to a former winner of the Miss Griffin Rock pageant who has a tiny dog named Poopsie that gets into all sorts of trouble. Mayor Luskey is quick to take credit for good ideas and blame others for bad ones.

Huxley Prescott will do anything to get the scoop. This journalist and TV reporter never goes anywhere without a microphone and his floating camera. Huxley believes aliens exist on Earth, which means he is always ready to report when the Rescue Bots leap into action!

Dr. Thaddeus Morocco

Dr. Thaddeus Morocco is a long-lived evil genius who menaces the Rescue Bots. He became friends and science partners with the famous author Jules Verne in 1862. Verne shared his "Verne Device" with Dr. Morocco, who used it to extend his life and travel through time.

Dr. Morocco commands a personal army of MorBots. MorBots are shape-shifting robots with cannon arms, rocket boots, and an armored tank mode. Dr. Morocco once traveled back in time and took control of Griffin Rock using his MorBots. Luckily, the Rescue Bots defeated him and reset the timeline.

Madeline Pynch and Priscilla Pynch & Myles and Evan

Madeline Pynch is a rich businesswoman who values money over people and the environment. She wants to drill for oil and mine for gold under Griffin Rock. She once teamed up with Dr. Morocco to force the Rescue Bots to work for her!

Madeline's spoiled daughter, Priscilla Pynch, uses her mother's money to buy her way through life and bully her classmates Cody Burns and Frankie Greene. At least she was somewhat thankful when the Rescue Bots saved her from the ravenous plants in the Sky Forest.

Griffin Rock's resident thieves are two brothers named Myles and Evan. Myles is a talented hacker. He uses his skills to break into the science labs on the island. Evan rarely speaks, but when he does, it is usually in grunts. No matter what schemes they plan, the Rescue Bots are always around to return the stolen goods and enforce the law!

Colonel Quint Quarry & Vigil

Colonel Quint Quarry is a hi-tech hunter who uses advanced tools to catch his prey. He owns the Quarry Safariland, his "playground" off the coast of Maine. When Optimus Prime turned into a feral Dino Bot, Colonel Quarry captured the Autobot leader and set him free in Safariland to practice his hunting skills. The Rescue Bots cured Optimus and helped Chief Burns arrest Colonel Quarry!

When Griffin Rock's main computer crashed, Mayor Luskey brought in the supercomputer Vigil to take over. Despite Doc Greene's warnings, Mayor Luskey gave Vigil full control of the island. Vigil overstepped its primary directive and took the whole town prisoner! Cody Burns saved everyone by tricking Vigil into frying its own systems.

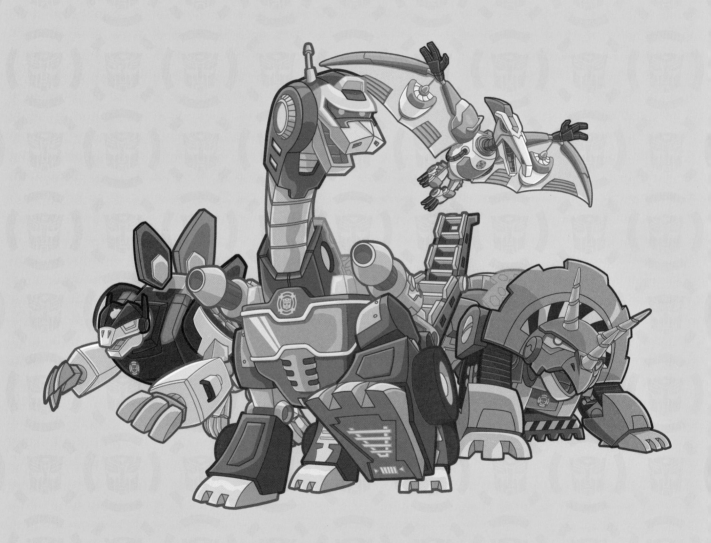

SERVE & PROTECT

A routine patrol with four Bots in stasis,
Years later awoke in the strangest of places.
Earth was their home now and in addition,
Optimus Prime gave them this mission:

"Learn from the humans, serve and protect,
Live in their world, earn their respect.
A family of heroes will be your allies,
To others remain robots in disguise."

Rescue Bots, roll to the rescue,
Humans in need, heroes indeed.
Rescue Bots, roll to the rescue, Rescue Bots.

With Cody to guide them and show them the way,
Rescue Bots will be saving the day.

Rescue Bots, roll to the rescue,
Rescue Bots.

The Ghosts of Griffin Rock

Adapted by John Sazaklis
Based on the episode "The Haunting of Griffin Rock"
written by Steve Aranguren

LITTLE, BROWN & COMPANY
LB kids

It is a dark and stormy night. Jerry is driving an armored truck full of money down a winding road along the edge of a cliff. With a crash of thunder and a flash of lightning, the glowing figure of a woman appears!

She floats toward the truck and whispers in an eerie voice, "Come home to me...."

Scared, Jerry swerves, and the armored truck plows into a guardrail, flinging the driver into the water below.

The Rescue Bots respond to Jerry's distress call. Dani and Blades find the driver clinging to a rock on the surf. They carry him to safety.

"Can you tell us what happened?" Chief Burns asks.

"It was the Lady of Griffin Rock!" Jerry exclaims.

Kade scoffs and says, "Have you had your eyes checked lately?"

Later that night, Cody tells Frankie about the rescue. "Who's the Lady of Griffin Rock?" he asks.

"Her name was Charlotte Wayne. Two hundred years ago, her husband and son were lost at sea," Frankie answers in a spooky voice. "Legend says that Charlotte's ghost is still looking for her family."

"Whoa." Cody gulps.

The next day, the emergency line rings. Chief Burns answers it, then says, "There's a ghost at the bank scaring away the customers."

The team exchanges concerned looks. Something spooky is happening in Griffin Rock.

"That's great!" Frankie exclaims. "It's the perfect opportunity to test my dad's Spectral Vapor Filters. They're designed to catch ghosts!"

"Rescue Bots," commands Heatwave, "roll to the rescue!"

The Rescue Bots arrive at the bank. The lobby is empty.

"See? I told you," Kade says. "There's no such thing as ghosts. We're just wasting our time."

Suddenly, a specter materializes before them. "Follow me!" it beckons.

"After that phantom!" cries Chief Burns.

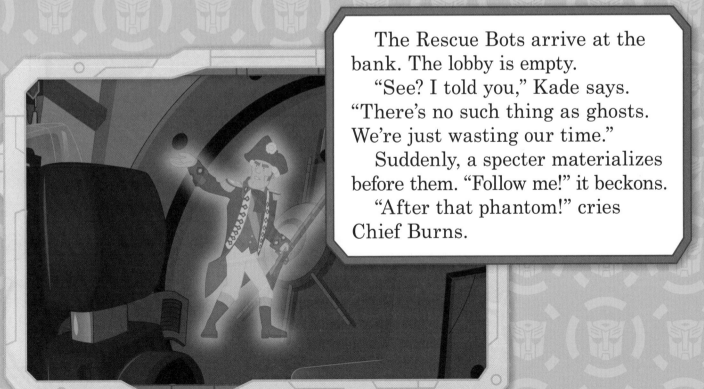

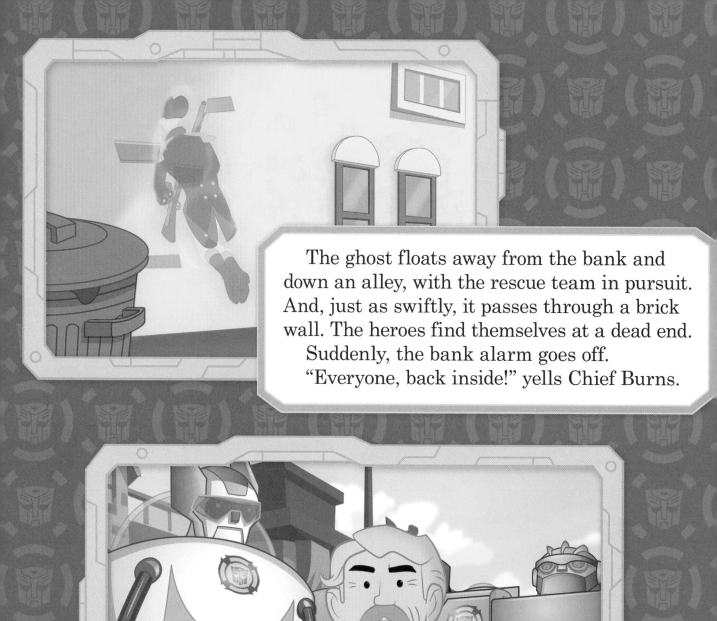

The ghost floats away from the bank and down an alley, with the rescue team in pursuit. And, just as swiftly, it passes through a brick wall. The heroes find themselves at a dead end. Suddenly, the bank alarm goes off.

"Everyone, back inside!" yells Chief Burns.

Chief Burns and his team race to the large vault. The contents have been completely cleared!

"How did that ghost empty the vault?" Boulder asks. "We were right behind it!"

"It didn't," answers the chief. "Ghosts can't steal."

The team deduces that the ghost was really a distraction, but they still don't know who, or what, the actual culprit is.

Cody's voice crackles over the Com-Link. "Guys, there are a lot of weird calls coming in," he says.

"Tell me it's not another ghost," replies Dani.

"Okay," says Cody. "It's a whole *lot* of other ghosts!"

Cody relays that there have been many more ghost sightings. Citizens are fleeing for their lives!

Chief Burns and the Rescue Bots are seeing ghosts, too, but they still can't believe their eyes!

Heatwave and Kade rush to a restaurant that has gone up in flames.

"Finally," says Kade. "An emergency I know how to handle!"

Kade grabs a nearby hose and blasts the blaze until the fire is out.

The firefighter and the Autobot enter the restaurant and make a discovery. "Fire's out, but the register has been robbed," Kade says into his Com-Link.

At that moment, Doc Greene arrives downtown with Cody and Frankie. "How do we stop the ghosts?" Graham asks.

"Allow me," Doc Greene replies. He pulls out his Spectral Vapor Filter and activates it. An energy field zaps one of the ghosts, causing it to fizzle and fade.

"That ghost is toast!" Frankie cheers.

But the victory is short-lived because the ghost reappears.

"Hmm," says Doc Greene. "My readings show that this is not a ghost—it's a hologram!"

The team goes to Doc Greene's lab. After some quick research, they learn that the holograms are coming from different projectors throughout the city.

"The signal is originating from the jail," the scientist says.

On the screen is an image of brothers Evan and Myles. "Ghosts can't steal," Cody says, "but those two do it for a living!"

Chief Burns heads to the police station and finds the two prisoners inside their cell. They are pacing back and forth, but the chief notices they haven't touched their food. As he enters, one of the prisoners passes right through him.

"The brothers must have escaped and hacked into the computer system," cries Chief Burns. "They built holograms of themselves to fool us!"

Another alarm blares.

Now a jewelry store is the target. Chief Burns contacts his team and tells them where the burglars are striking.

"It's time to put an end to this ghost story!" he says.

The Rescue Bots roll out to the scene of the crime.

   Meanwhile, the two brothers are in the jewelry store filling up their burlap bags with expensive items.

   "That police chief and his team of tin cans aren't as smart as we are." Evan laughs.

   "Yeah," Myles agrees. "Thanks to our dirty little trick, we're picking this city clean."

As Evan and Myles make their escape, they come face-to-face with the law.

"Halt, burglars," cries Chase. "We have you surrounded!"

But the brothers do not stop. They run through the legs of the robots as fast as they can.

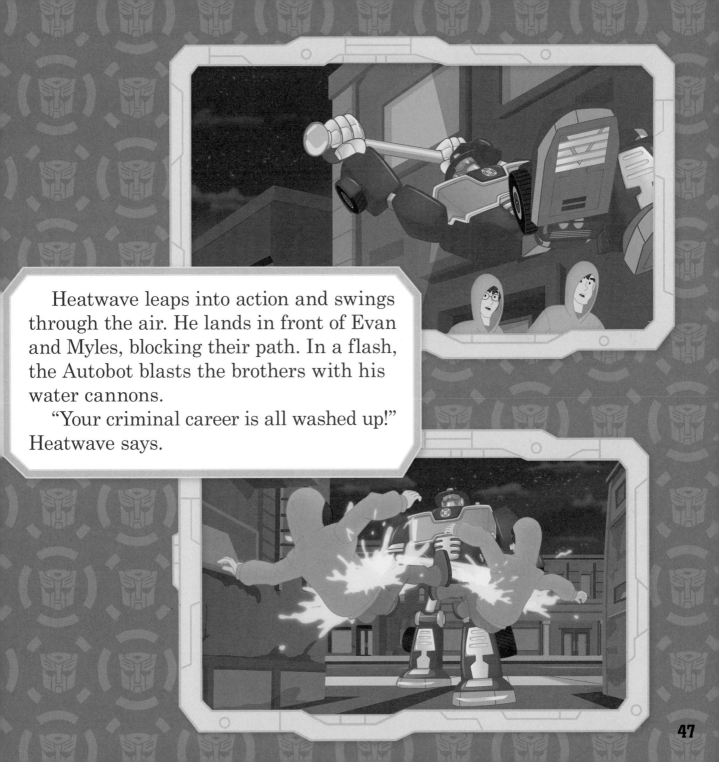

Heatwave leaps into action and swings through the air. He lands in front of Evan and Myles, blocking their path. In a flash, the Autobot blasts the brothers with his water cannons.

"Your criminal career is all washed up!" Heatwave says.

While Chase and Chief Burns take the brothers back to jail, Kade turns to the others and says, "Looks like the hauntings were a hoax after all."

Suddenly, the Lady of Griffin Rock appears and cries, "Come home to me!"

Kade jumps with fright. "Was that a hologram or a ghost?!"

Cody smiles and says, "We'll never know!"

Land Before Prime

Adapted by John Sazaklis
Based on the episode "Land Before Prime"
written by Nicole Dubuc

LB kids

It's another regular day for the Rescue Bots and the humans patrolling Griffin Rock. Blades and Dani are scanning the skies when they come across something very strange—a pterodactyl!

"Aaaaah!" Blades cries. "Is that what I think it is?"

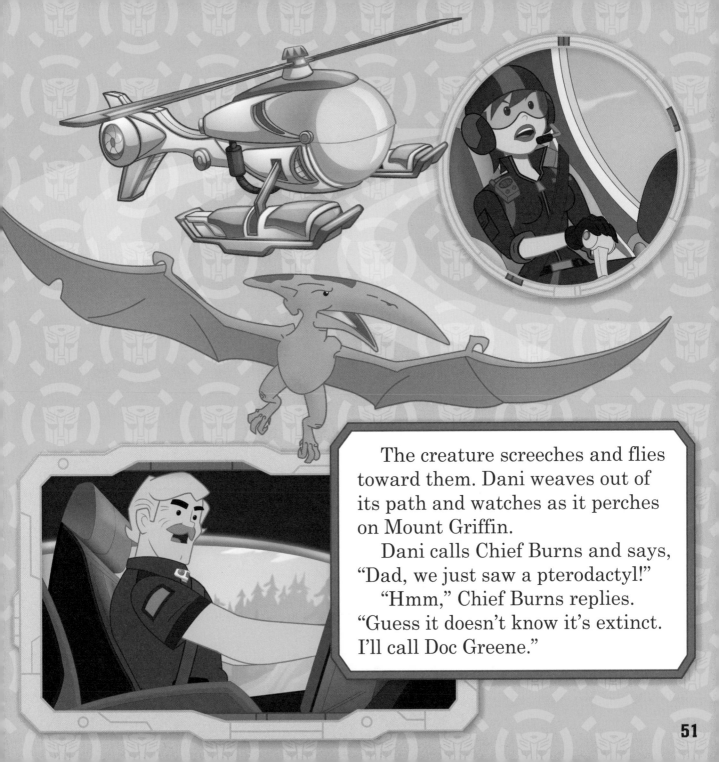

The creature screeches and flies toward them. Dani weaves out of its path and watches as it perches on Mount Griffin.

Dani calls Chief Burns and says, "Dad, we just saw a pterodactyl!"

"Hmm," Chief Burns replies. "Guess it doesn't know it's extinct. I'll call Doc Greene."

At the firehouse, Graham explains where the winged reptile came from. "A chain of explosions opened deep sinkholes beneath Griffin Rock," he says. "It's possible one of them reached as far down as the prehistoric caverns. There must be life within!"

The Com-Link beeps with an incoming message. It's Doc Greene. He is flying alongside the pterodactyl with a hang glider!

"This is amazing!" he exclaims. "I've never imagined seeing one of these up close!"

"When I said to observe that thing, I meant with a telescope!" Chief Burns says. "So, what's the plan?"

"We'll cage the pterodactyl long enough to place a tracker on her," Doc Greene says. "After she's released, we can follow her and make sure she gets home safely. My guess is that she's nesting."

The Rescue Bots follow the scientist's orders. They meet Doc Greene at Mount Griffin. Blades has a cage dangling from his winch. He drops it over the creature.

After putting a tracking device on the pterodactyl, they free her from the cage. "She's headed toward Wayward Island. That's where the subterranean rift must be located," says Graham.

"I would be happy to search for the passage myself," Doc Greene says.

"It's dangerous, Doc," Chief Burns says.

"I'll take Trex with me. What's a more logical bodyguard than a robotic dinosaur?"

Doc Greene, Trex, Kade, and Heatwave head toward Wayward Island. They soon reach the coast and pull up to the shore.

"I wonder if there really are dinosaurs on the island," Kade says.

"Only one way to find out," says Doc Greene. "We'll be back soon."

The doctor and the dino bot head deep into the dense jungle. When they reach a clearing, they see an astounding sight—real live dinosaurs!

"Great thunder lizards!" shouts Doc Greene.

A large tyrannosaur sees Doc Greene and charges at him! Trex tries to help but gets trapped by falling rocks!

While running away, Doc Greene gets lost in the jungle-like plants. He stops to catch his breath and hears a sound among the trees.

At first, he thinks Trex has escaped from the rockslide. But it's the real tyrannosaur roaring with rage!

Heatwave springs into action and sprays the dinosaur with his water blasters. "Back off, scaly!" he shouts.

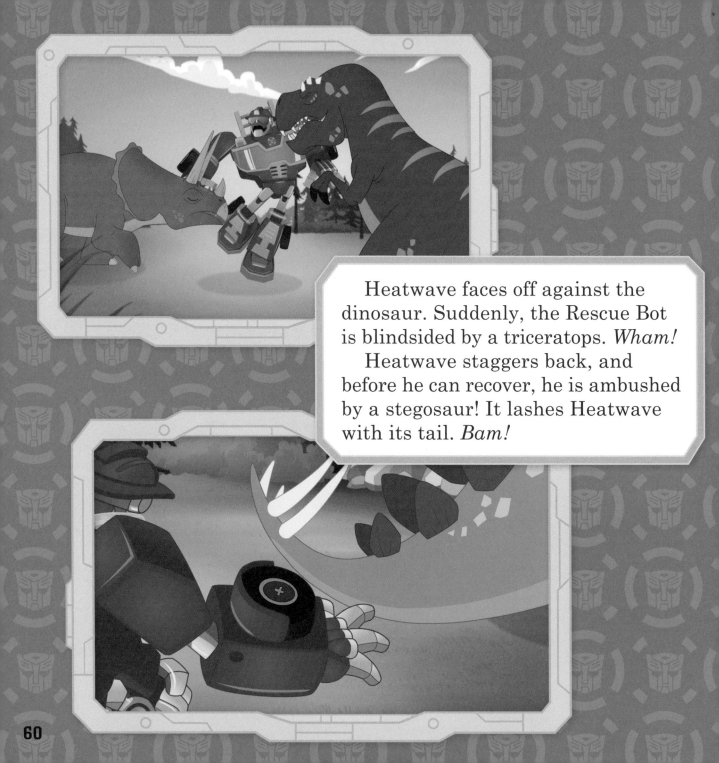

Heatwave faces off against the dinosaur. Suddenly, the Rescue Bot is blindsided by a triceratops. *Wham!*

Heatwave staggers back, and before he can recover, he is ambushed by a stegosaur! It lashes Heatwave with its tail. *Bam!*

The dinosaurs have surrounded the Autobot.

"Time to make tracks," Heatwave says. He changes into fire-truck mode. "Hop in, Doc, before those things smash me into fossil fuel!"

Doc Greene jumps into the moving vehicle, and Heatwave races back to the shore.

Meanwhile, Optimus Prime arrives at headquarters. "I heard about the subterranean passage and came to oversee the mission," he says. "Those dinosaurs could have been living underground for millions of years!"

All of a sudden, a distress call from Kade comes in. "The dinosaurs are acting up, and we're in trouble!" he says.

Optimus Prime deploys the rest of the team. "Rescue Bots, roll to the rescue!" he commands. Only he and Cody stay behind.

Once the entire team arrives at Wayward Island, Heatwave and Doc Greene lead them into the jungle.

"The dinosaurs tried to enter the passage, but a rockslide occurred," says Doc Greene. "Trex is trapped under some boulders. We have to save him and help the dinosaurs get home!"

The heroes find Trex, but as soon as they approach, they hear a terrible roar!

The tyrannosaur has returned, and he's brought his friends along for another fight!

"Stop! We're trying to help you!" cries Heatwave as a brachiosaur slams him into the ground. A triceratops locks its horns with Boulder, a stegosaur gets ready to slam Chase, and the pterodactyl stalks Blades.

"Fall back and regroup!" Heatwave shouts. The Rescue Bots change into vehicles and retreat from the rumble.

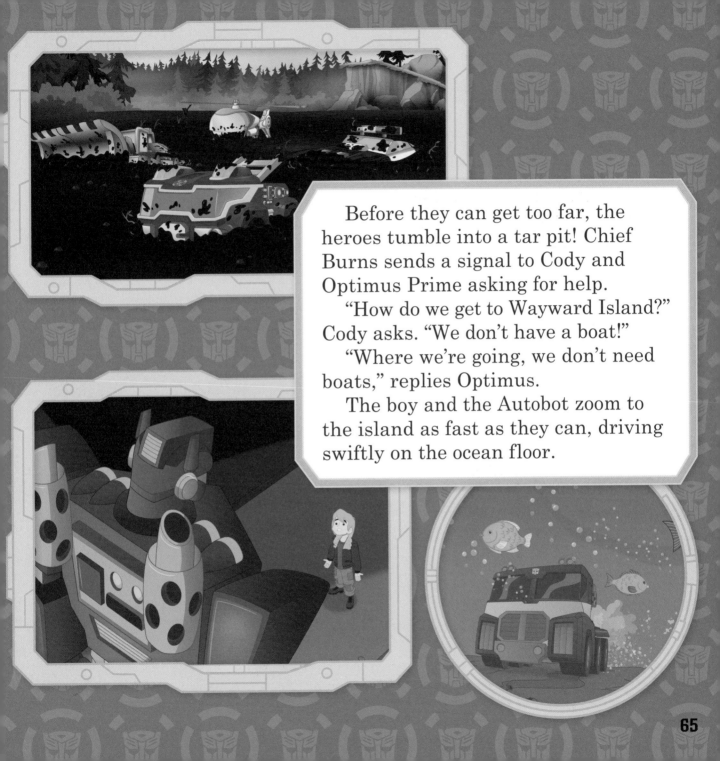

Before they can get too far, the heroes tumble into a tar pit! Chief Burns sends a signal to Cody and Optimus Prime asking for help.

"How do we get to Wayward Island?" Cody asks. "We don't have a boat!"

"Where we're going, we don't need boats," replies Optimus.

The boy and the Autobot zoom to the island as fast as they can, driving swiftly on the ocean floor.

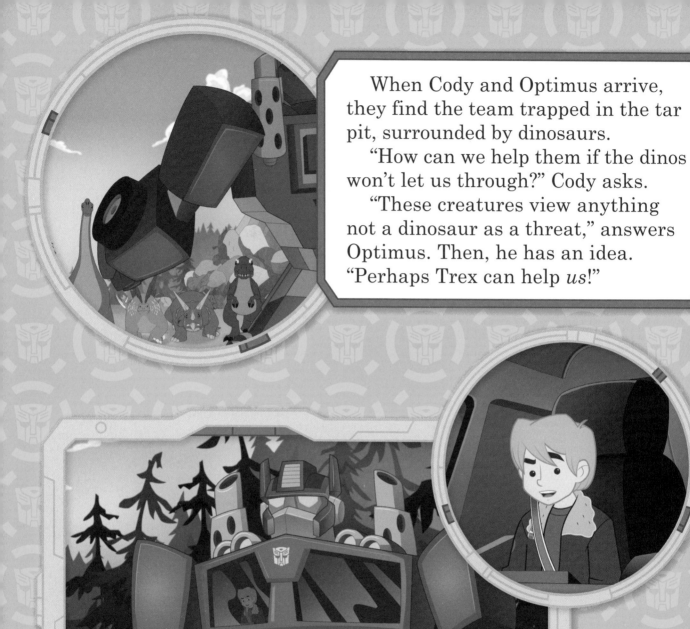

When Cody and Optimus arrive, they find the team trapped in the tar pit, surrounded by dinosaurs.

"How can we help them if the dinos won't let us through?" Cody asks.

"These creatures view anything not a dinosaur as a threat," answers Optimus. Then, he has an idea. "Perhaps Trex can help *us*!"

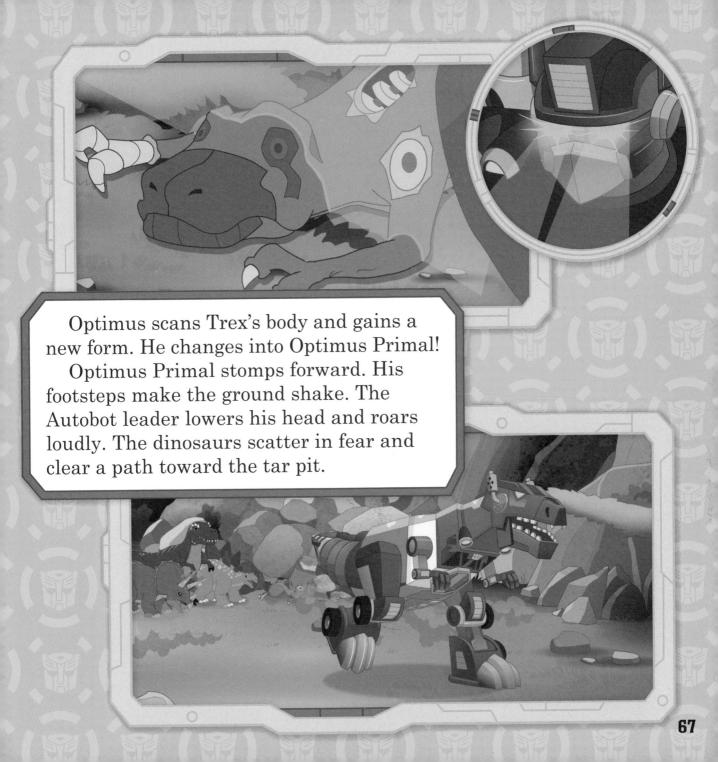

Optimus scans Trex's body and gains a new form. He changes into Optimus Primal! Optimus Primal stomps forward. His footsteps make the ground shake. The Autobot leader lowers his head and roars loudly. The dinosaurs scatter in fear and clear a path toward the tar pit.

Blades, Boulder, Chase, and Heatwave continue to sink deeper and deeper into the tar. All seems lost until Optimus Primal rushes to the rescue! He grabs Chase's bumper in his massive jaws first. Then the other Bots are slowly pulled free.

Chief Burns thanks Optimus for his assistance. "That was one sticky situation," he says.

Together, the team returns to free Trex. Using his new powers, Optimus Primal unleashes a sonic roar. The massive sound waves blast the rocks into tiny pieces. Trex is free, and the underground passage is open once again!

The team then makes a startling discovery—a nest full of baby dinosaurs!

"This explains why the creatures emerged," says Optimus Primal. "They were foraging for food for their young."

"They are *so* cute!" Kade squeals. "Just look at 'em!"

"Let's seal up that crack so they can stay safe underground again," Graham says. Together, the Rescue Bots and their friends move the boulders back into place.

"Everyone to the boat," says Chief Burns when they are finished. "It's time this mission became prehistory!"

Blast Off!

Adapted by Lucy Rosen
Based on the episode "Space Bots"
written by Greg Johnson

LITTLE, BROWN & COMPANY
LB kids

"Today's the big day!" Cody beams at his brother Graham. "In a few minutes, you and Doc Greene will be hurtling through space on a laser-powered elevator. Aren't you excited?"

"Sure," Graham says. "I'm excited. In a terrified sort of way."

"Come on," says Cody. "The *Asgard* is an amazing machine. You'll go straight up and come right back down. It's no big deal."

"It's time to go," says Professor Anna Baranova. She invented the *Asgard* so that scientists could easily study the galaxies from outer space. "Once you get to the top, you'll have a whole week to conduct tests and research!" she says.

Doc Greene gives his daughter, Frankie, a hug, and Graham says good-bye to the Burns family.

The Burns family and Frankie hang out on the sidelines to watch the *Asgard* take off.

"T-minus ten seconds to liftoff," the control tower announces. "Ten...nine...eight..."

"Here they go!" cries Cody.

But there's something blocking the path of the laser!

"Rescue Bots, roll out!" yells Chief Burns.

"We're on it!" exclaims Heatwave. The robots leap into action.

"Seven...six...five..."

Boulder, Blades, and Chase grab hold of the spacecraft and lift it off the ground.

"Four...three...two..."

"Hurry," says Professor Baranova. "If they don't remove the obstruction, the laser will overload!"

"One!"

With no time to lose, Heatwave leaps to swat the object out of the way.

"Blast off!"

The laser powers up and lifts the *Asgard* into the sky.

Later that night, the four Rescue Bots and Cody sit on the rooftop, while Frankie uses her telescope to search for signs of the *Asgard*.

"Maybe one of us should have gone with Doc and Graham—in case something else goes wrong," says Heatwave.

"Guys!" cries Frankie. "I see it! Check this out." She shows everyone the *Asgard* and its flight path in space.

But Cody is distracted. "What's that?" he asks, zooming in on a streak of light in the corner of the screen.

"It's a meteor," says Frankie. "Daddy has been tracking it for weeks. It's not on course to go anywhere near the *Asgard*."

"It's headed for *something*, though...." Heatwave murmurs to himself. "But what?"

On board the *Asgard*, Graham and Doc Greene go through their checklist. Doc Greene calls out the names of the *Asgard*'s four pods as Graham looks at each of them on his computer screen.

"Everything is stable!" exclaims Doc Greene. "That means we did it! Phase one is complete."

But before Graham can even breathe a sigh of relief, the *Asgard*'s alarm begins to blare.

"What's happening?" asks Graham.

On Earth, the gang watches the meteor through Frankie's telescope. It tears through space, blasts through an asteroid field, and sends a huge rock careening toward the *Asgard*!

"The asteroid is heading straight for one of the ship's four pods!" yells Frankie. "If it hits, the whole machine will be unstable! We've got to do something—quick!"

In space, Doc Greene and Graham prepare for impact. *Boom!* The rock wipes out the *Asgard*'s living quarters pod and knocks the ship off course!

No one is hurt, but now the *Asgard* is floating through darkness with no way to get back on course. The radio is down. Graham and Doc Greene can't get in touch with anyone on Earth.

"What do we do now?" Graham whispers nervously.

"We wait for a rescue," says Doc Greene.

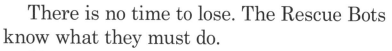

There is no time to lose. The Rescue Bots know what they must do.

"Rescue Bots, get ready," says Chase. "Looks like we're about to go on a space rescue!"

Cody and Frankie get Chief Burns. Together, the humans and the Rescue Bots head to a secret hangar, where the ship the Bots came to Earth in is hidden.

"The *Sigma*," Boulder marvels. "Think we remember how to fly her?"

"We're about to find out," says Heatwave. "Boulder, Chase, you're copilots. Everyone, strap in. It's time to rocket to the rescue!"

The *Sigma*'s engines roar. The ship lurches forward. With a blast, the spacecraft takes off into the dark night sky.

"Wow, Cody," says Frankie. "Don't you wish we were going, too?"

No one answers.

"Cody?" Frankie looks around. "Where is he?"

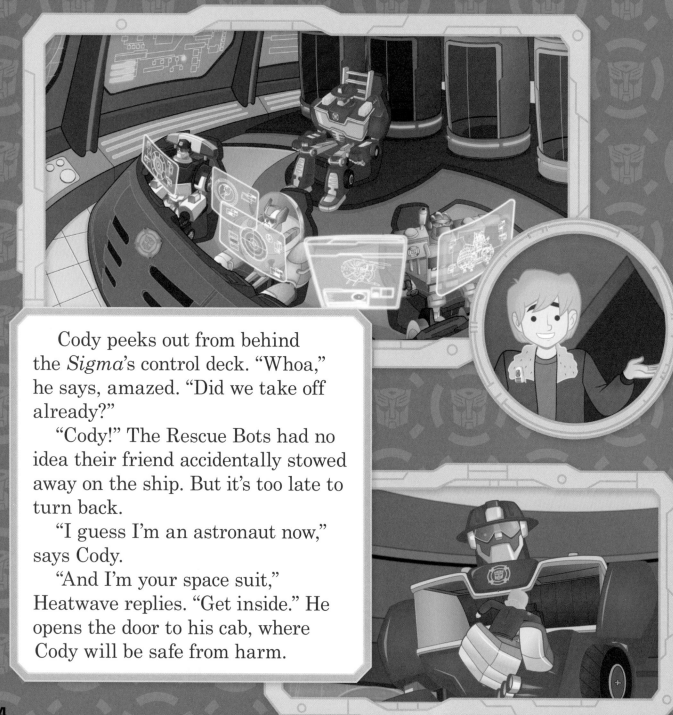

Cody peeks out from behind the *Sigma*'s control deck. "Whoa," he says, amazed. "Did we take off already?"

"Cody!" The Rescue Bots had no idea their friend accidentally stowed away on the ship. But it's too late to turn back.

"I guess I'm an astronaut now," says Cody.

"And I'm your space suit," Heatwave replies. "Get inside." He opens the door to his cab, where Cody will be safe from harm.

The *Sigma* climbs higher into space. Soon enough, the *Asgard* is just within reach.

"Boulder, move us closer," Heatwave commands. "I'll go get Doc and Graham."

As he pushes down the *Sigma*'s entry ramp, Heatwave speaks to his friend. "Buckle up, Cody," he says. "Looks like you're going on a space walk."

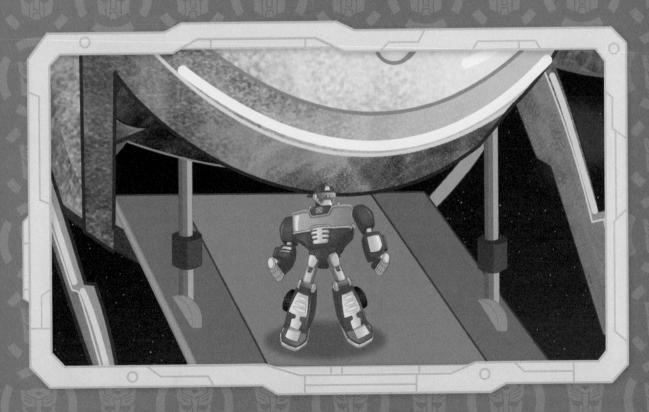

With a swift leap, Heatwave propels himself at just the right angle. His momentum carries him straight to the *Asgard*! As soon as he reaches the ship, Heatwave tears through each pod, searching for his friends. At last, he finds Graham and Doc Greene huddled in the greenhouse. "Get in!" he commands.

Heatwave is just in time. A split second after Doc Greene and Graham close the door to Heatwave's cab, the greenhouse's windows crack open—sucking all the air out of the pod!

"Hold on!" Heatwave yells as all the oxygen pours out of the ship, knocking him off his feet. Heatwave grabs at anything he can, but the suction is too powerful. He is pulled into space!

"We're adrift," Heatwave signals to his friends aboard the *Sigma*. "I don't have any propulsion."

"Now what do we do?" cries Blades in despair. "We did not train for this!"

"Keep calm, everyone," Heatwave says. "We'll think of something."

Just then, Cody has an idea. "Use your fire hoses," he says. "If you spray them, the force of the water will push us in the right direction!"

"Worth a shot," says Heatwave. "Here goes nothing." In a flash, Heatwave activates his water reserves. The burst of water sends the Rescue Bot flying!

"It's working!" Graham cries.

Once they're back aboard the *Sigma*, the Rescue Bots hitch the *Asgard* to their spaceship.

"Looks like we got everything we came for," says Boulder. "Next stop—Griffin Rock!"

The gang lands back on Earth in no time.

"Daddy!" Frankie rushes to Doc Greene's side.

"Welcome back, son," Chief Burns says to Graham.

"You had us worried," Dani tells him.

Everyone is so relieved to see the space travelers back home safe and sound. Even Kade gives Graham a hug!

"Well, Rescue Bots," says Blades, "it looks like our space rescue was a success."

"Yes," says Boulder. "And it was kind of nice flying the *Sigma* again!"

"Perhaps we'll get the opportunity to use her again someday," Chase remarks.

"Maybe," Heatwave says. "But nothing beats rolling to the rescue on good old terra firma."

"What is that?" asks Boulder. "Earth?"

Heatwave looks at the night sky. He looks around at his friends on Griffin Rock. At last, he speaks. "It's home."

Race to the Rescue

Adapted by Steve Foxe
Based on the episode "The Need for Speed"
written by Mairghread Scott

LITTLE, BROWN & COMPANY
LB kids

The Rescue Bots are a group of Transformers who protect and serve the humans of Griffin Rock.

Heatwave leads the team. Chase, Blades, and Boulder are part of the original crew, while Blurr is one of the new recruits!

Heatwave needs Blurr's help with an emergency. Kade is stuck in the middle of a toxic waste spill! Blurr rushes to the rescue.

"Slow down!" Heatwave shouts.

But it's too late for Blurr to stop.

The Autobot spins out of control and splashes toxic sludge all over Kade! Blurr panics—until he sees Kade smile and eat some of the goo. It's not toxic waste—it's cake frosting!

"This was a surprise test," Heatwave explains. "You did not pass."

Blurr gets frustrated. He doesn't like being tricked. He changes into a race car and speeds away.

As he zooms through the streets of Griffin Rock, Blurr finds graffiti written in Cybertronian. The Autobot follows the sound of spray painting nearby and spots a strange figure in the shadows.

"Another test already, Heatwave?" Blurr asks. "I will not fail again!" He calls for backup and races off to catch the criminal.

Blurr chases the round Bot through the streets and right into an Autobot ambush!

"It's a Mini-Con!" Boulder says. Heatwave tries to blast the menace with his nozzles, but the Mini-Con spits water back into Heatwave's face!

The Mini-Con, named Bounce, smashes through a nearby truck and spills laughing gas into the streets!

"We'll deal with the gas," Heatwave says to Blurr. "You go catch that Con!"

Blurr shifts into high gear. Out of nowhere, a red sports car knocks Blurr off the road!

"No way is a human stealing my rescue," Blurr says.

But the red sports car isn't being driven by a human—it changes into an Autobot!

"Time for you to go back to jail, Bounce!" the red Autobot shouts at the Mini-Con.

When Blurr finally catches up, he is confused to see Bounce with another Autobot. The red stranger mistakes Blurr for a Decepticon and launches a flying kick!

While the two Autobots fight, Bounce escapes!

Heatwave and the other Rescue Bots arrive and recognize the red Autobot.

"You're Sideswipe," Blades says.

"You're a member of Bumblebee's team!" says Heatwave.

With the confusion cleared up, the Autobots return to the firehouse. Sideswipe explains that Bounce escaped custody and jumped through a Groundbridge to Earth.

Blurr is jealous that Sideswipe chases after criminals instead of waiting around to rescue humans in danger.

"Maybe you should join Bumblebee's team," Sideswipe says. "If you're fast enough to catch Bounce, that is."

"You can decide your place after the mission," Heatwave says. "Rescue Bots, roll to the rescue!"

The team sets up a trap to catch Bounce. But it's up to Sideswipe and Blurr to trick the Mini-Con into getting caught.

Bounce leads the Bots on a high-speed chase. Blurr skids out of control and nearly crashes into a crowded café!

Luckily, Sideswipe tackles Blurr at the last second, saving the people. But Bounce escapes into the sewers.

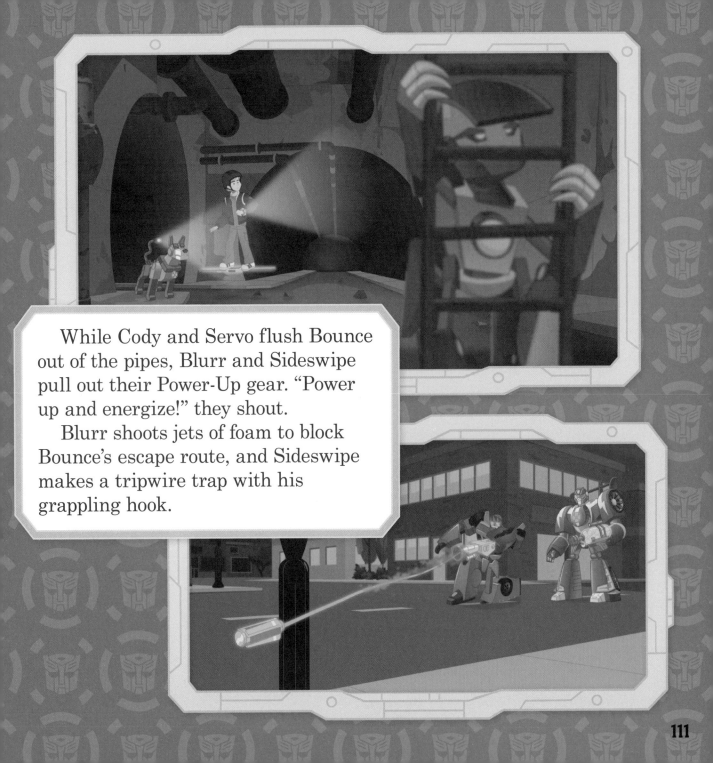

While Cody and Servo flush Bounce out of the pipes, Blurr and Sideswipe pull out their Power-Up gear. "Power up and energize!" they shout.

Blurr shoots jets of foam to block Bounce's escape route, and Sideswipe makes a tripwire trap with his grappling hook.

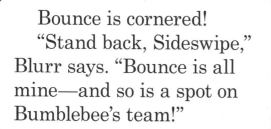

Bounce is cornered!
"Stand back, Sideswipe," Blurr says. "Bounce is all mine—and so is a spot on Bumblebee's team!"

Before Blurr can nab the Mini-Con, Bounce knocks over a lamppost, which starts to fall toward a human!

"Look out!" Blurr yells. The speedy Autobot abandons his pursuit of Bounce and rescues the innocent human from harm.

Just then, a speeding car turns the corner! Blurr acts fast and stops the vehicle with his foam gear as the other Rescue Bots capture Bounce.

Blurr feels like a failure. "I missed my one shot to join Bumblebee's squad," Blurr says.

But Heatwave claps Blurr on the back. "That's because you're a natural-born rescuer!" he says. "You just saved two humans without even thinking!"

Blurr feels better. After some thought, he makes up his mind. "I am not sure I can go any faster than I do now," Blurr says, "but I know that if I train harder, I can become a better Rescue Bot!"

Dangerous Rescue

Adapted by Brandon T. Snider
Based on the episode "Endangered Species"
written by Andrew Robinson

LITTLE, BROWN & COMPANY
LB kids

One beautiful spring day, Cody, Frankie, and Kade join their Rescue Bot friend Boulder for some bird-watching in the park.

Kade sighs. "Only Boulder could enjoy a pastime that even *humans* know is boring."

"I find the variety and beauty of Earth birds to be inspiring. Cybertron doesn't have anything like this," explains Boulder. He checks his bird-watcher book.

"That one is a woodpecker, and she has *babies*!" whispers Boulder. Cody and Frankie climb to a high branch so they can get a better look.

"Hey, kids! Climb down from there! It doesn't look safe," says Kade. Suddenly, the tree branch snaps, and Cody and Frankie start to tumble toward the baby birds.

"Power up and energize!" says Boulder, springing into action. He catches the kids in one hand and uses his laser to slice away the tree branch with the other.

"Are the baby birds okay?" asks Frankie. The tiny creatures hop onto Boulder's hand.

"They're wonderful," Boulder says, smiling. The mother bird hops onto Boulder's head and gently pecks him. "Hey, that tickles!"

Back at the firehouse, Doc Greene explains the meaning behind Boulder's discovery. "That's the first golden-crested woodpecker anyone has seen in forty years. We mustn't tell anyone about this. These birds need to be protected as an endangered species. The worst possible thing would be a crowd of tourists trampling through their habitat."

"What's an endangered species?" asks Boulder.

"An endangered species is an animal that's in danger of becoming extinct," answers Doc Greene. "If we can get those birds on the endangered species list, the government will step in to protect them."

Boulder loves protecting humans, but he thinks the birds should be kept safe, too.

Boulder talks with Chief Burns about the birds' safety. "Our mission is to serve and protect humans. But what about those creatures who need protection *from* humans?" he asks. "Those baby birds need guarding until Doc Greene can get them on the list."

But Chief Burns has concerns about the Rescue Bots protecting the birds full-time.

"I'll allow it on *one* condition: You can't neglect your *real* jobs," says the chief.

"Great!" exclaims Boulder, but not all the Rescue Bots want to be part of Boulder's mission.

"Our job is keeping people safe, not birds," grumbles Heatwave. "Count me out."

The next day, everyone else heads to Woodpecker's Grove to stand guard. Boulder suggests they clean up the area and plant some new flowers. He thinks the birds might like something pretty and fresh. The flowers attract a swarm of bees! Boulder has to plant the flowers a bit farther away.

Boulder thinks some nice, soothing
music would calm the birds down
after all the activity. He and Blades
play some music, but it's too loud. The
birds are even more frightened. Blades
fumbles with the controls until he is
able to lower the volume. Chief Burns
stops by to see how things are going.
He is surprised.

"I didn't realize your plan to protect the woodpeckers included scaring them," jokes Chief Burns.

Soon the babies come out of their hiding place. They look like they are ready to fly. Blades has some advice for the little birds. "Do what I did the first time. Just close your eyes and scream." Blades laughs.

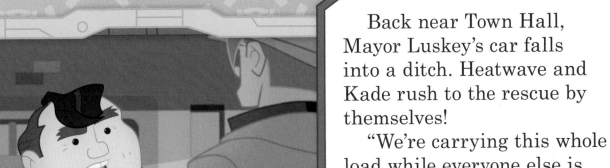

Back near Town Hall, Mayor Luskey's car falls into a ditch. Heatwave and Kade rush to the rescue by themselves!

"We're carrying this whole load while everyone else is babysitting. Those birds don't look so endangered to me," says Kade.

"Did you say *endangered*?" asks Mayor Luskey.

Kade is in trouble now. No one is supposed to know about the birds.

"As mayor, I order you to come clean!" says Mayor Luskey.

"I, uh, *heard* there's a family of golden-crested woodpeckers that everyone thinks are extinct. But it's a secret. *Please* don't say anything," Kade pleads.

"Don't worry, my boy. I know how to keep a secret," says Mayor Luskey.

Heatwave changes into his vehicle mode. Kade hops in, and they drive away. Mayor Luskey smiles and waves as they depart.

Mayor Luskey makes a phone call. "Get out your floaties, because we're about to be swimming in tourists." He is up to something.

Later, the Rescue Bots and Cody watch as the mayor makes a big proclamation on the steps of Town Hall. "I'm thrilled to announce the rediscovery of the golden-crested woodpecker, right here in Griffin Rock!" says Mayor Luskey.

Cody can't believe what he is hearing. How did the mayor find out about the birds?

Cody gets a call later from reporter Huxley Prescott demanding to know who discovered the birds and where they are located. Boulder disguises his voice and handles the situation. He tells Huxley that the birds need to be left alone.

"That's the end of that," Boulder says, hanging up the phone. But he is wrong.

The next day, Huxley persuades Kade to disclose the location of the birds' nest. Then the mayor turns the spotlight on himself yet again. He announces where the woodpeckers are living.

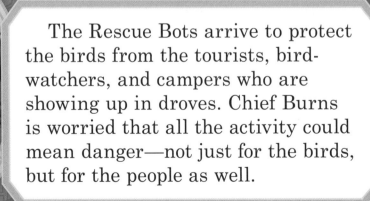

The Rescue Bots arrive to protect the birds from the tourists, bird-watchers, and campers who are showing up in droves. Chief Burns is worried that all the activity could mean danger—not just for the birds, but for the people as well.

Oh no! An out-of-control campfire causes sparks to fly into Woodpecker's Grove!

Quickly, the Rescue Bots roll into action and help the people get to safety. Blades uses his scoop claw to douse the fire from above.

When Heatwave arrives, he blasts the flames on the ground.

Boulder shovels dirt onto the fire. The Bots put the fire out!

The townsfolk are saved! But the birds flew away during the commotion. Luckily, Doc Greene tagged them so he could track their location.

"I am sure the birds will return to their home in no time," says Doc Greene.

"Perhaps there's a way the birds can be safe and a way for people to still see them?" wonders Cody. That gives Doc Greene an idea.